Martin's MRI

Wendy J. Hall

Martin enjoys doing sports very much. As soon as the bell rings for recess, he hurries to get to the basketball court. He meets his friends there and they play together.

One day, he was in such a hurry to get down the stairs that he tripped and tumbled down a few flights.

He hit his head very hard on one of the steps. His head was cut open and blood was pouring from it. His friends went to get the school nurse.

They took him to the nurse's room and she stopped the bleeding and cleaned and dressed his wound.

"I feel dizzy," said Martin.

The school nurse called Martin's mom to come and pick him up. She advised her to take him to the hospital or to see a doctor to check him over.

Martin's mom took him straight to see Dr. Daniel. Dr. Daniel looked at his head. He had a big bump where he had fallen.

"Do you have a headache or feel like you want to vomit?" asked Dr. Daniel.

"Yes, I do have a headache and my eyes feel blurry," Martin replied.

"I think it would be best for you to have an MRI to look inside your head and make sure everything is fine inside because your vision is blurry. It looks like you have a pretty bad bump there."

"What's an MRI?" asked Martin.

"Nurse Nina will tell you all about it and I'll have the results back quickly.

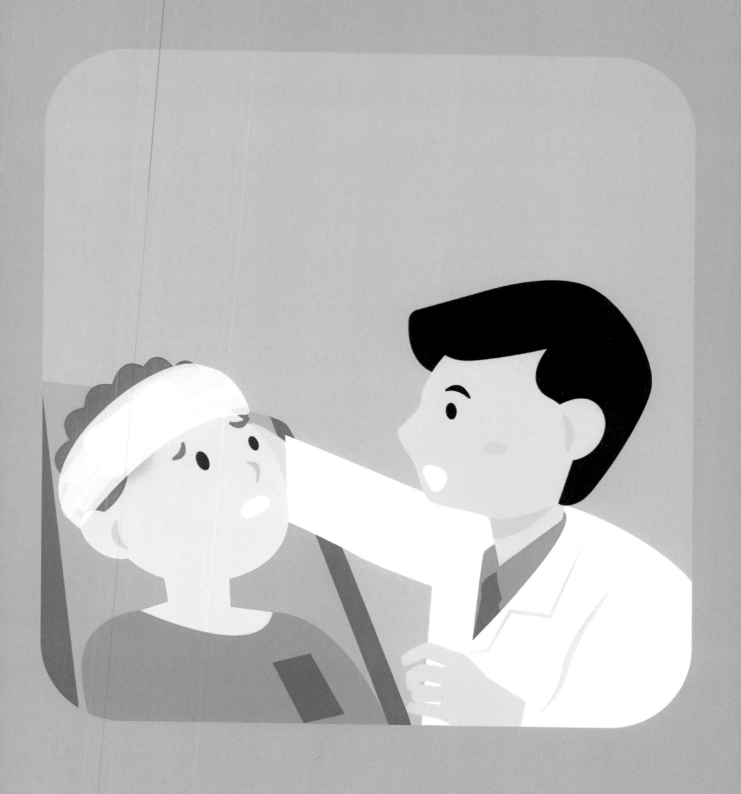

"There's nothing to be afraid of," said Dr. Daniel.

Nurse Nina got a wheelchair because Martin felt dizzy and then she took him to her room to prepare him for having an MRI scan. Martin was glad he didn't have to walk.

Once they got to her room, she told him about MRI scanners and how they work. Martin felt interested.

"MRI stands for Magnetic Resonance Imaging. That's a lot of words to remember. It's like a big donut with a tunnel inside it.

"You lie on a bed and it moves in and out of the scanner, taking pictures of your brain in tiny slices. It has a giant magnet inside it."

She also told him that sometimes a needle had to be put into a vein for some special medicine called "contrast" to help the doctor see very clearly and that the needle hurt a little.

Daniel looked scared.

"You don't need to worry though, because Dr. Daniel said you don't need contrast."

Daniel was relieved.

"I need to tell you a few things about the MRI scanner.

"First, you'll have to lie very still in the scanner or the pictures won't be clear. The scanner also makes a lot of loud noises so you'll be given some special headphones to wear and you can listen to some music.

"The technician will place a special cage over your head to keep it in the right position. You don't need to be scared and you'll have a special button to press if you do.

"Some MRI scanners even have mirrors, so you can see the technician behind the window looking at your brain on big computer screens."

"Wow! That sounds cool. I wish I could see inside my brain," said Martin.

Nurse Nina wheeled Martin to the MRI waiting area and helped him change into a special gown.

He went into the MRI room and the technician checked to make sure he didn't have any metal on his body. She helped him to lie down on the table.

The technician put headphones on for him and put his head into a special cage so he could keep it still.

Martin's heart was beating fast and he felt afraid. The technician told him to relax and that it would be over quickly. She gave him a button to press if he felt really afraid.

Martin decided that he would be brave.

The technician told him they were starting and the bed started to move like magic into the tunnel.

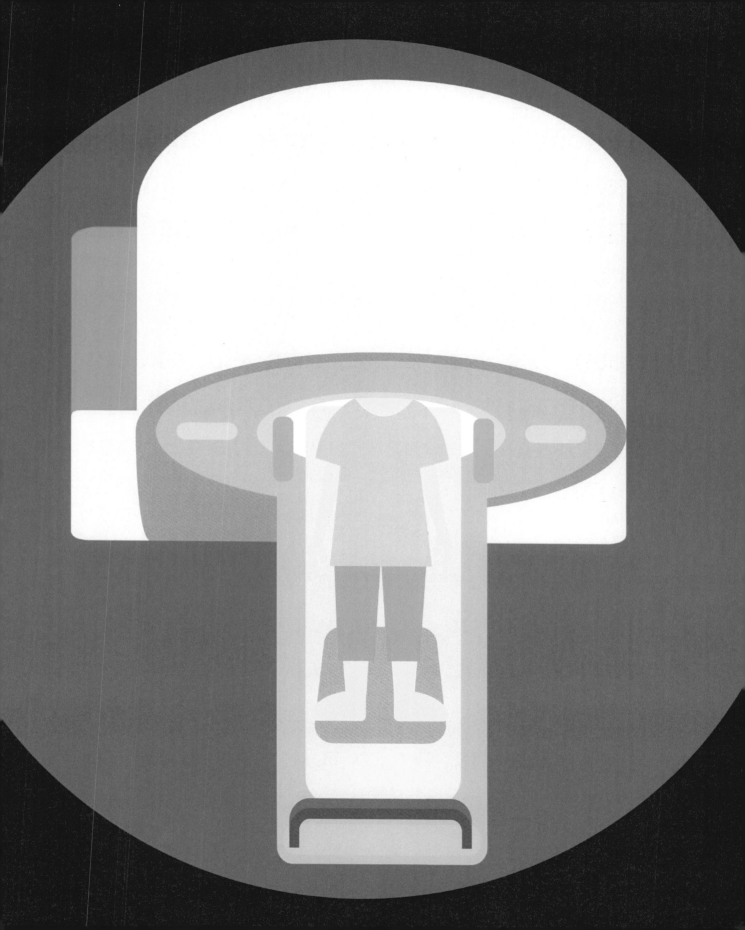

Martin heard the noises but they weren't too loud as he could hear the music through the headphones. He lay very still.

Soon, the technician came in and said it was all over. She gave him a sticker that said, "I am brave." He felt very happy.

Martin and his mom waited for half an hour and then were called back into Dr. Daniel's room.

"I'm very happy to tell you that your MRI is normal. There is no bleeding inside. You can go home and rest.

I AM

BRAVE

Dr. Daniel gave Martin's mom a special information leaflet that told her to keep a watch on him, and if he began to vomit or have any other symptoms to come straight back to the hospital.

Martin's mom was very relieved to hear that he hadn't hurt his head inside.

For his science project presentation, Martin decided he would talk about the different imaging scanners in hospitals.

He did some research and learned about the difference between X-rays, CAT (CT) scans and MRI scans.

He made a computer slide show to show his class.

"X-rays take simple photos and mainly show your bones," he said. "They use something called radiation, which is not good for our bodies.

"CAT (CT) scans are like X-rays and use radiation but the pictures are more detailed as it takes them slice by slice.

"You lie inside a donut, but it doesn't have a tunnel. Sometimes you need a special needle in your arm to put some medicine in to make the pictures clearer for the doctor to see.

X-ray

CAT Scan

MRI Scan

"Finally, MRI scans give the most detail and let the doctors see your body parts in 3D. They don't use radiation but you sometimes need a needle with special medicine, too.

"All of these scans are painless and actually quite fun if you learn about how they work."

Martin's class enjoyed the presentation very much and clapped loudly.

Martin felt very proud.

About the Author

Originally from the UK, Wendy speaks five languages and has authored over 100 educational books. The inspiration for this innovative series comes from personal experience: Her own daughter, then aged eight, once spent a year in hospital and underwent major surgery.

While taking care of a scared child, Wendy could not find materials that helped her navigate the healthcare system. This situation kindled a dream: to provide parents and medical professionals with a tool to make medical procedures, illnesses, and adverse childhood circumstances less frightening.

Wendy has extensive knowledge of the medical field as she herself suffers from a rare, chronic illness. An award-winning Patient Leader, she works to improve healthcare by advocating and educating.

To learn more about Wendy, please visit the website:

https://www.mediwonderland.com

31380862R00018

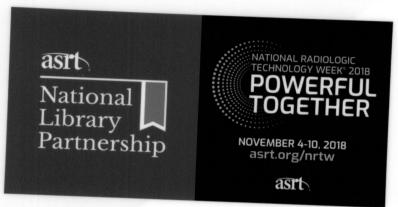

This book is donated by the American Society of Radiologic Technologists. Radiologic technologists are the medical professionals who perform diagnostic imaging examinations, administer radiation therapy treatments and provide patients with high-quality care.

Learn more at asrt.org
#ASRTLovesLibraries.

Wendy J Hall
Visit the website at
https://www.mediwonderland.com/

First Printing: December 2017
Mediwonderland

ISBN-13: 978-1981232437